D0429328

To Catch a Mugger

Margaret Scariano

A PERSPECTIVES BOOK
High Noon Books
Novato, California

Series Editor: Penn Mullin
Cover Design: Sue Rother
Illustrations: Herb Heidinger

International Standard Book Number: 0-87879-298-8

6 5 4 3 2 1 0 9 8 7
8 7 6 5 4 3 2 1 0 9

Contents

CONTENTS

CHAPTER 1

The Mugger

It was almost dark. Russell Newley crossed the street. A week ago he had moved from New York to San Francisco. He hoped to find work on the West Coast. Work at the warehouse in New York had been slow. Russell had been laid off from his job as janitor.

So far in San Francisco he hadn't even found a part-time job. In New York he'd had friends. But here, he was no one. Even worse, he was no one and had no money.

Russell stood watching the cars and trucks go by. The sidewalks were empty now that the stores were closed. Then Russell saw an old woman crossing the street towards him. Boy! She was asking for it. Just begging to be ripped off. Russell saw her purse hanging from her arm. What an easy target for a purse-snatcher! As she walked past him, Russell couldn't help laughing

1

at her. She wore a felt hat decorated with droopy flowers, a man's jacket, and bedroom slippers. What a sight!

Russell remembered Bob, the guy across the hall from him at the rooming house here in San Francisco. Russell had asked him about work and he'd said, "Work? What's that? Need money? Mug someone." Then he'd laughed.

Now Russell looked again at the old woman. This was his chance. He really had to get some money. He noticed that halfway down the block there was an alley — a fast way to get out of sight! He walked a little faster so that he was almost behind the old woman. He looked around to be sure they were alone on the street. Taking a deep breath, he broke into a run. It was just like Bob had said. The run by the person, the snatch, the getaway. Man! What a power trip. He felt great!

Now he was even with the old woman. Russell reached out, snatching at the purse. But the old woman didn't let go of her purse.

"Thief! Thief!" she screamed.

Russell then started to pull at the purse. His hands were wet with sweat.

"Let go, will you!" he yelled, still jerking at the purse.

"Mugger! Help! Help! Police!" She screamed

like an alley cat.

Russell was scared by the old woman's cries. He pushed his hip into her side. Yelling with pain, she fell on the sidewalk. Her purse flew through the air and landed on the sidewalk. Russell grabbed the purse and ran toward the alley. Once he turned into the alley, he knew he was safe. Now he leaned against the brick walls

"Help! Help! Police!" She screamed like an alley cat.

3

of the building. His heart pounded. He could hear her screaming. Under a light, Russell dumped out the stuff from her purse. He threw away the usual things in a woman's purse—the comb, tissues, keys. He picked up the wallet and emptied it. Seven dollars! That's all. Just seven dollars! Then he tossed the purse aside, too. The seven dollars he stuffed into his pocket.

Russell could hear the woman moaning on the sidewalk. He peeked around the corner of the alley. Someone *must* have heard her. Why weren't they coming to help? What's the matter with people? Giving the empty purse a kick, he headed down the alley. But he couldn't forget her cries.

What was wrong with him? He'd done just what the guy said and got seven dollars. No big deal. At least it would buy him something to eat. But he'd never hurt anyone before. He slowed his walk. Maybe he'd check one more time to see that someone was helping the old lady. Russell went back to the alley entrance. He peeked around the corner again. She still lay there, alone. He could see people up in the apartments. Maybe no one wanted to get mixed up in this. He couldn't just leave the old lady there on the sidewalk. He decided to act as if he were just out for a walk and happened to see her.

Russell walked down the street toward the old woman. He started to whistle. When he reached her, he bent down beside her.

"What happened?" he asked. "Did you fall?" How smart he was, acting like he didn't know.

"Who is it? Don't hurt me! Please." The old woman grabbed his jacket.

"I won't hurt you. I want to help," Russell said. He almost laughed out loud.

"My glasses. I can't find my glasses," the old woman cried.

Russell looked around and saw them a few feet from her. One side was broken, the other cracked. He handed them to her.

"Can't see anything with these," she said.

"Can you sit up?" Russell asked.

"It's my arm. I think it's broken."

Then he heard the sirens. A few minutes later he saw the flashing lights.

It was too late to run. But he was safe. The old lady couldn't tell he was the mugger without her glasses.

As the officer stepped from the police car, Russell said, "I'm glad you're here. This poor old lady's been mugged!"

CHAPTER 2

Trapped

The policeman stood beside the old woman. Then he looked at Russell. "Who are you? Her son? A friend?"

Russell said, "No. No. Listen, I don't know her. I'm just your everyday good citizen out for a walk. I just happened to see her, man. That's all."

The policeman nodded. "I have some questions. Would you mind waiting for a few minutes?"

"That's cool," Russell said. "I can wait."

By this time the other policeman was out of the car. He stood right behind Russell.

"I've called for an ambulance," the policeman behind Russell said.

The other one bent down beside the woman. "Where do you hurt?"

"My arm. The guy broke it."

"You mean the person who stole your purse?" the officer asked.

"Of course, I mean that, you fool." She began to cry.

"Your name?" The policeman had his pad and pencil out.

"Glass." She sniffed. "Mrs. Joseph Glass."

"Well, Mrs. Glass, would you know this man if you saw him again?" the policeman asked.

"That mugger, you mean?" Her voice got hard. "Yes, I'd know him. But a lot of good it does. Without my glasses, I wouldn't know my own cat."

Now Russell felt good. He didn't feel so tight now. This was OK. He was smart—smarter than any of them. He spoke up. "I found her glasses on the sidewalk and gave them to her, but they were broken."

The police officers looked at each other. Russell had the feeling that the policemen knew something he didn't. He didn't have the smart feeling he'd had a minute ago. Had he said too much? Now he wished he'd said nothing. In fact, he wished he'd never gone back to the old woman. What was that old saying? "A criminal always goes back to the scene of his crime." But that was in the old days, wasn't it? Surely these two officers wouldn't think he did it—the one who stopped to help.

"Did you try to hold onto your purse, Mrs. Glass? Did you fight the mugger for it?"

"You bet I did. He has no right to my money."

Then one of the policemen went to the car and brought back a blanket to cover the woman. The other questioned Russell. Name? Address? Place of work?

"No job? How do you live?" the policeman asked, writing down Russell's answers.

"My life's savings. Brought the cash with me from New York," Russell said.

The officer turned to the old woman. "How much money did you have in your purse?"

"Seven dollars," she answered.

Now they stood by the car. "Empty your pockets, Mr. Newly. Put everything on the hood of the car."

Russell lined up some nickels and quarters on the hood, also a pocket knife and a comb. From his other pocket he pulled out the seven dollars.

"Hmmm. Seven dollars. That's just what Mrs. Glass had stolen," the officer said.

"Hey, man, she's not the only one who has seven bucks. Mine looks the same as hers."

"No, it doesn't," Mrs. Glass said. "My five

dollar bill has 'Reno' written in red ink on top of it. It's my lucky five."

The policeman held the five dollar bill. He shone his flashlight on it. Sure enough, "Reno" stood out like a sign at the top. It might be her lucky bill but it sure wasn't Russell's. He felt like someone had just hit him in the gut.

The policeman held the door of the car open. Russell climbed in. They didn't even turn on their siren, but took him to jail quietly. Not a bit like on TV. These policemen acted like it was no big deal taking him in. But Russell thought it was a very big deal indeed.

Russell was questioned and finger-printed. Then he was booked and put into a large cell. Inside were lots of bunks filled with men. Russell took an empty bunk. Then he sat down. Imagine, me in jail with these bums, Russell thought. The smell of the place was terrible. He pulled the blanket over his face.

CHAPTER 3

The Sentence

The next morning Russell had to be in court.

"How do you plead?" the judge asked him.

"Guilty." Russell was glad his New York gang wouldn't hear about this.

Then Russell's lawyer and the judge talked. Finally the judge said, "I've been looking over the report, Mr. Newly. You are guilty of no other crimes. You went back to help Mrs. Glass. Because of this, I suggest six months' probation and 200 hours of community service."

"OK, Judge." Russell didn't have any idea what community service meant, but at least he wouldn't be in jail.

"Now, before you think you're getting a great deal, let me explain." The judge leaned back in his chair. "Probation means that you will report to the probation office every week. You will talk over any of your problems with the probation officer. Do you understand?"

"Yes, Judge." This was going to be easy, Russell thought.

"Now as to community service. I will tell you about the volunteer jobs that are open. You can then choose where you want to serve your 200 hours. First, the park always needs good weeders. How are you on weeding?" The judge pulled his glasses down on his nose. He looked over them at Russell.

Weeding. That sounded like the pits. Why he'd be bent up like a pin after 200 hours, Russell thought.

"I grew up in New York City. I don't know about weeds."

"I understand, Mr. Newly. Here is something else. The city can use a volunteer to pick up litter from the sidewalk. Being from the city, Mr. Newly, you do know litter, I'm sure."

Russell groaned inside. "Yes, Judge." He remembered seeing these men in New York. They carried long poles with a nail at the end. They walked around picking up scraps of paper on the sidewalks. There must be something else he could do. He'd do anything but that!

"Or think about this. We have a new volunteer group called the Citizens' Convoy. A volunteer rides the same bus each day. His job is to help old people get on and off the bus and keep kids from fooling around. He is to report any strange people to the police."

"You mean I could do my 200 hours of community service just by riding the bus?" Russell asked. He saw himself in the back of the bus with his feet up, enjoying the ride.

"Yes, by riding the bus and doing the things I said," the judge said.

"Do I carry a gun?" Russell asked.

The judge stood up. "No. You do not carry a gun! You wear a shirt with the words 'Citizens' Convoy' across its back. Now which of these would you like to do, Mr. Newly?"

Russell quickly said, "The Citizens' Convoy, Judge." At least he could sit while he gave his 200 hours to the community.

"Fine, Mr. Newly. One other thing. They tell me you've paid two weeks' rent for your room." He looked at the report on his desk. "You told the officer you didn't have a job and were living off your life's savings.

"Well, Mr. Newly, just so you won't have to use too much of your life savings to eat, we have a job for you. It will be at the City Center Coffee Shop as a dishwasher. You will ride the bus for two hours in the morning during rush hours. Then you'll work at the coffee shop for a few hours. Again during the afternoon rush hours, you will ride the bus home. Any questions?"

"Yes, Judge. How much does the dishwasher job pay?"

"Your food and a couple of dollars an hour."

A couple of dollars! That was the pits. Maybe he'd just sit it out in jail. Figure it was like a paid vacation. His friends in New York would never know.

"If you do not take any of these service jobs," the judge said, "you'll have to spend six months in jail. The work there is digging ditches."

Quickly Russell said, "That Citizens' Convoy sounds fine to me, Judge."

"I thought it would. Now do a good job, or, Mr. Newly, do *hard* time in jail."

CHAPTER 4

Citizens' Convoy

It was Russell's first morning on the Citizens' Convoy. "Nothing to the job, Russell," said another volunteer, an older man. "You're here to help people. Just seeing a guy in a Citizens' Convoy shirt makes people feel safe. You'll get to know the regular riders. Think you can handle it?"

"No problem," Russell said. He thought that 200 hours of community service was going to seem twice as long as a life sentence.

"Good luck." The volunteer shook Russell's hand. "You'll do just fine. I can tell you know a lot about people. Just the way you look at each rider shows you're interested."

By the end of the week Russell was tired of the whole deal. He had done twenty hours of Citizens' Convoy work. By this time, he knew all the regular riders and exactly what each one would say every morning. The man who owned the Five and Dime store always said, "Good morning, Citizen Russell. Another day and another dime, as we say in the business." Then he'd laugh all the way to his seat.

And Mrs. Hanley, the nurse, answered Russell's "How are you?" the same each morning. "As well as can be expected."

The waitress, Gloria, never smiled. Russell thought her face looked like a mask. She barely moved her lips so she wouldn't get wrinkles. "Morning," she said.

But the guy who really bothered Russell was the man with the little round cap on his head and glasses. Each morning this man laid a fancy saying on Russell. Today he'd said, "Russell, riding the bus is just like life. Every so often there's a bump or a bridge to cross over."

After his morning ride, Russell actually looked forward to his dishwashing job. At least he didn't have to listen to dumb jokes or stupid sayings.

On Monday of his second week, it happened. Russell was standing outside the bus waiting for the regular passengers to get on. Suddenly a girl hopped on the bus and greeted the driver.

"How was the vacation, Darcy?" the driver asked.

"Fine. I just laid in the sun and soaked up the rays," she said.

Russell thought she was the prettiest girl he had ever seen. And—was he lucky! She worked at the City Center Coffee Shop! Instead of going to the kitchen to get his coffee, Russell got it at the counter. He paid for it, and Darcy handed him his change. "Thank you," she smiled and then said, "Oh, you're with Citizens' Convoy. I'm Darcy Jones."

"Russell Newly."

"I'm so glad you're on the bus every day, Russell. I feel much safer." Darcy said.

Just let some dude bother her on the bus. I'll show him a thing or two, Russell thought. He said, "I'll make sure you'll be safe on the bus, Darcy." Then he headed for the kitchen and all the dishes waiting to be washed. All afternoon he thought of Darcy. He could hardly wait for the afternoon bus ride to begin.

The day had been hot for San Francisco. The passengers going home seemed tired. The bus hadn't gone a block when a fight broke out between two twelve-year-old boys. First, it was just words. Then one of the boys shoved the other. The nurse screamed. The man in the cap hit both boys with his umbrella. Without making a

16

wrinkle in her face, the waitress moved her lips. "Fight. Fight."

Now both kids were rolling and tumbling, hitting and pounding. Russell grabbed one boy's arm and put his foot on the other. "Knock it off, guys. This is a bus, not a playground." Russell had heard a school bus driver say that once. It sounded right. He sat one boy in an empty seat in the back and the other up front near the driver. Then Russell walked to where Darcy sat. "Are you all right?"

"Oh, yes. I was afraid they would hurt each other — or you, Russell."

Right then Russell knew that he had to take Darcy out. Maybe for pizza and a movie. He figured up his dishwashing pay. He'd made forty dollars last week. But out of that, he'd had to pay for his room. His savings were going fast. He had to do something. Or else how could he take Darcy out?

CHAPTER 5

Meeting with Bob

Take Darcy out. Take Darcy out. Russell kept on thinking about it. He liked her. He thought she liked him. But where could he get money? He wasn't making much at the dishwashing job. In fact, he just made enough to pay for his room.

As he was lying there on his bed that night at the rooming house, Bob banged at the door. Bob! He was the guy who had told him how easy it was to get money fast. Look where it landed him!

"Who's there?" Russell yelled.

"Who else? Me," Bob called back.

Russell got up and opened the door. Bob came and laid down on the bed.

"Make yourself at home," Russell said.

"That is what I'm doing, buddy," Bob said. "What's new? I haven't seen much of you."

"No, you haven't. After getting caught over

that old lady, I was put on the Citizens' Convoy," Russell said.

"Citizens' Convoy? *That* thing?" Bob said. He sat up. "Man, you've got to be kidding."

"No, I'm not, Bob. It's OK. You should try it, too," Russell said.

"Me?" he asked.

"That's what I said—*you*," Russell said. "Look, Bob, you've been lucky. But your luck is going to run out. It's no good to keep on going after money that isn't yours. That poor lady had only seven dollars. I don't want to take money from people who don't have it."

"Wait a minute. Are you telling me you have a job?" Bob asked.

"Sure I do. It isn't much right now. But I get my meals—good ones—and enough to pay for this room," Russell said.

"Is that all, man?" Bob said.

"And," Russell said, "I have a girl friend!"

"Man, that's great," Bob said, "but do you have enough bread to take her out?"

"Well, now," Russell answered, "that's a problem."

"I knew it! I knew it! You want to hit me up for some bread. Right?" Bob said.

This made Russell stop for a minute. What if

Bob did give him some money? How would he pay him back?

"Well, a few bucks would help me out," Russell said.

"OK, I'll tell you what. We'll both pick up a few bucks," Bob said.

Something didn't sound right in the way Bob said that. "What do you mean?" Russell asked.

"Well," Bob said, "we'll just find ourselves another little old lady."

Russell was thinking about Darcy. She liked him. She wouldn't want to see him if he got into trouble like that. She didn't know he had already been in trouble. If he was caught, he wouldn't see any more of Darcy.

"Forget it, Bob," Russell said. "I'll take care of things myself."

"Well, OK, man. I was just trying to help," Bob said. He got off the bed and started for the door.

"Bob, come along with me — just one day on the Citizens' Convoy," Russell said. "You'll like it."

"No way. No way," Bob said. He left the room.

Money. How was Russell going to get money to take Darcy out?

CHAPTER 6

The Next Day

Russell left the next morning to start his job on the bus. The regular passengers got on. By this time each one knew Russell and said something to him. Then Darcy got on. She always smiled. It made Russell happy just to see her. They sat together in the back of the bus. Darcy could tell that Russell had something on his mind.

The bus pulled to a stop. Russell hopped off to help the passengers. He held out his hand to help one lady get on. Then he saw it. Her large purse was wide open! Russell saw her wallet inside. It lay beside a pack of cigarettes and a paper bag. The woman was not a regular passenger. She was very neatly dressed and had blue-grey hair. She wore lots of gold bracelets above her white gloves. Russell was sure her wallet had money. Lots of it. It would be so easy to take her wallet. He could have lots of fun with that money.

Russell sat down and thought about all the places he could take Darcy. The lady wasn't even thinking about her purse. It was on the seat beside her, wide open. Suddenly she jumped up.

"That's my stop!" she yelled to the bus driver. Her purse fell to the floor. She picked it up and hurried off the bus.

The lady was gone. Russell couldn't believe it. He'd been having such fun thinking about that money. Then he saw something on the floor. It was under the seat she had just left. It was the paper bag. It must have fallen out of her big purse. Could be her lunch, he thought. Forget it. He looked out the window. There was the lady, heading down the street. She was still close by.

Russell surprised himself. "I'll get off at the corner," he called to the driver. He grabbed the paper bag and ran towards the door. The bag felt heavy. He jumped off the bus at the corner. Then he started back after the lady. She had gotten pretty far down the street. Russell went running after her. When he got close to her, the lady turned around. She must have thought he was chasing her to get her money. Russell could see the scared look on her face.

"Your paper bag!" he shouted. He held out the bag, but she had already turned around. She started to run. Suddenly she tripped. Down she went on the sidewalk. Then she just lay there.

Russell was scared. He had to get away. Fast. No one would believe that he wasn't trying to mug the lady. He ran. Then he ducked into an alley. He leaned up against a brick wall. He felt stupid. Why did he chase after that lady anyway—just for an old lunch bag? He dropped the bag on the ground. And now the police would be all over the place. He could hear the sirens. He kicked the paper bag. It opened up. Russell saw something green inside. He bent down and dumped out the bag. Money! Rolls of it all tied up! His fingers shook as he counted out the bills—$9500! This couldn't be happening to him—Russell Newly!

There was something else in the bag—a small black book. Inside there were a lot of names. Sums of money were written by each name. Russell's heart pounded. The names on the list were the names of *gamblers*! And gambling was against the law. The white-gloved lady was a bookie! Russell was sure of it!
Here he was in another big mess, and he had only been trying to help.

Russell just stood there for a few minutes. Thoughts were racing through his head. He

Money! Rolls of it all tied up! He counted out $9500!

could just walk away and leave the bag and forget the whole thing. He could take the money and get out of town fast. Well, I've got to do something, he thought. I'll go back to my room and hide the money and then maybe I can come up with a plan.

CHAPTER 7

Fear

Russell put the money and black book back into the paper bag. Then he put the bag inside his shirt. He looked like he was wearing a pillow. Peeking out of the alley, he saw no one on the street. All he wanted to do was get back to his rooming house. He started to run. He was sure someone was following him. His heart pounding, Russell got to his room and leaned against the door. He put a chair under the doorknob.

Every noise in the old rooming house scared him. He listened. Was someone—someone from the Mob—coming to get him? He knew the first thing that lady bookie would do. She'd call Mob headquarters to tell them she'd been ripped off. And she'd gotten a good look at Russell—both on the bus and when he chased her. When he'd yelled "Your paper bag," she had thought he was after her bag of money. Now when she woke up and found the bag missing, she'd be sure he had taken it. The Mob didn't waste time. Russell knew they'd have someone looking for him.

All night long he tossed and turned in his bed. Every night sound made him worry. At dawn he knew what he'd have to do. He'd take the money with him to the bus. If he saw the lady bookie, he'd hand her the bag. He had to get rid of that money before the Mob got to him. But what if the lady never showed up?

Russell dressed for work. He put a belt around his waist next to his skin. Then he put the money under it. With his shirt loose, the money didn't show.

He was the first one at the bus stop. He greeted each person who got on. The Five and Dime man said, "Good morning, Citizen Russell. Another day, another dime, as we say in the business." Then he added, "You broke up a good fight yesterday. I was ready to bet on the red-haired kid. Ever do any betting, Russell?"

"No," Russell said quickly. His hand checked to be sure his shirt covered the belt and the money.

When the nurse got on, Russell asked, "How are you?" He expected her usual, "As well as can be expected." But Mrs. Hanley surprised him.

She said, looking at him closely, "How are you? You look a little pale. Something wrong?"

Gloria, the waitress, didn't even say her short, "Morning," but patted his arm as she took her seat. The man in the cap touched the glasses on his nose and leaned down close to Russell. "Riding the bus," he said, "is like a life of crime. Both roads are full of pot holes."

By the time Darcy got on the bus, Russell was in a cold sweat. He was sure the regular passengers knew about the bookie.

Darcy smiled at Russell as she climbed on and took her seat. She had a great smile, Russell thought. The money next to his skin didn't feel good. When Darcy waved to him to come to her seat, Russell wondered if he might keep just twenty dollars of the money. Then he could take Darcy out. It would be like a reward for returning the rest of the money. But did he dare not return all the money?

The bus pulled into the stop where the lady had gotten off yesterday. Russell looked for her. He hoped she'd get on, and he could get rid of the money. The two twelve-year-old boys climbed on. They sat way in the back.

Just as the bus driver closed the door, a man ran up and pounded on it. The door opened. The man got on and put money in the box. He looked down one side of the bus. Then he looked across the back and up the other row. When he saw Russell, he took the toothpick out of his mouth. He looked hard at Russell. Then he smiled. His two front teeth were gold.

Russell looked away. He didn't know which scared him more—the gold teeth or the man's smile.

Russell had to move. He walked up and down the bus. He could feel the man looking at him. But when he turned around, the man was looking at Darcy.

Russell felt a little better. Maybe the gold-toothed man wasn't from the Mob at all. Maybe he was checking on how well Russell was doing his community service. Or he could even be a new person riding the bus. Yeah. He was sweating over nothing, Russell told himself.

Now the gold-toothed man's eyes were on Russell, going over every part of him. The money around Russell's waist seemed to swell. It felt like a spare tire. Then Russell saw the scar on the man's cheek. It moved like a snake as the man's mouth twisted into a smile. The man's eyes seemed to say, "We know who you are."

CHAPTER 8

The Choice

That evening the gold-toothed man rode the bus again. This time he sat behind Darcy. When Russell got on, Darcy waved to him. She was sitting next to an older woman.

"Russell, I want you to meet my mother."

"What a good idea to have a Citizens' Convoy on the bus," Darcy's mother said. "There are so many street crimes. It's nice to know that Darcy is safe from muggers on the bus."

Russell couldn't even answer. He kept on walking. As he passed the gold-toothed man, Russell felt his X-ray look. Russell was sure the man could see his knees shaking and hear his heart pounding. He knew the man could see the money hidden around his middle. Russell hurried to the back of the bus.

When Darcy and her mother got off at their stop, the gold-toothed man left, too. As the bus pulled into traffic again, Russell fell back into an empty seat.

That night Russell put the money under his pillow. He didn't dream of Darcy and pizza and movies. In his sleep the gold-toothed man chased him and caught him, and shoved him against a building. When he aimed his gun at Russell, the man smiled and his gold teeth shone brightly in Russell's eyes. Suddenly, Russell woke up. The sun was shining in the window of his bedroom.

Russell quickly dressed for work. Again he hid the money around his waist. When the bus pulled into the stop, the driver said, "Russell, the head office called. You're to go to the probation office right away."

Russell was scared. Maybe the lady bookie had told the bus company that he had mugged her. Should he cut out? Make a run for it? But what chance did he have with the Mob *and* the police after him? He needed help. Would Darcy say they were together at the time? No. He didn't want Darcy to know. She'd never go out with him then.

The probation officer met Russell at the office. "Sit down, Mr. Newly. I understand you're doing a good job at the coffee shop and on the Citizens' Convoy."

Suddenly Russell felt terrific. This wasn't about a mugging after all. He held his hands so the money wouldn't show.

"We do have another mugging, though," the probation officer continued. "It was a lady on your bus." The probation officer was talking about the white-gloved lady. "She looks like someone's mother, Mr. Newly. But she isn't. She's a bookie and works for the Mob, and she says she lost a lot of their money."

Russell felt tight inside. Should he hand over the money? Would they believe him that he hadn't mugged her?

Then the officer said, "Her name is Mrs. Lawson. She's in St. Joseph's Hospital. She wasn't hurt, but she's sure scared. She knows how the Mob works. They don't like someone taking their money. So she's scared and says she's in a lot of pain. We're letting her stay in the hospital longer so that maybe she'll tell us something. Then we can arrest the Mob leaders."

"But it wasn't her fault that she lost the Mob's money," Russell said.

"Try telling that to the Mob. I feel sorry for whoever has the money. The Mob always gets them," the probation officer said.

Now Russell really felt scared. His shirt stuck

to his sweating chest. The money around his waist felt sticky.

"I'm telling you this, Mr. Newly, so you can keep your eyes open. Let us know if there are any strange-looking people on your bus. By now you know your regular people. Just keep watching closely. That's all."

Now Russell wondered if the gold-toothed man was a "spotter" or maybe a police under-cover man. He asked, "Do you have undercover guys riding the bus now?"

"No. We need all our people to handle the emergency calls." The probation officer stood up. "Keep up the good work, Mr. Newly." He walked Russell to the door.

For the first time in his life, Russell wished a policeman would say, "You're under arrest." At least then he'd be safe from the Mob. He dreaded seeing the gold-toothed man again. Now he knew he wasn't a "spotter" from the court or an under-cover cop. When Russell left the building, he kept looking around. He was glad no one was following him. He started to run. He ran around cars in the middle of the street and into an alley. Then he hid behind a trash can for a few minutes. He didn't see anyone so he headed for the coffee shop. It was too late for his morning community service bus ride.

He looked in the coffee shop window. Darcy was there. He decided to have coffee and a donut before he started his dishwashing job. It'd give him a chance to talk to Darcy. Sitting at the counter, Russell stirred his coffee round and round. Then he looked in the mirror behind the counter. There, standing not five feet behind him, was the gold-toothed man! He tried to drink his coffee. He couldn't. He got up quickly.

"Missed you this morning, Russell," Darcy said as he paid for the coffee.

The gold-toothed man sat at the counter now.

"Yeah. Had some business to do," Russell said. "See you on the bus tonight, Darcy." Then he walked fast to start his dishwashing job.

That night it rained. When Darcy got on the bus, the gold-toothed man got on right behind her. Had he sat all day at the coffee shop waiting for Russell to come out? The money felt heavy around Russell's waist.

The people on the bus seemed tired this evening. It was quiet except for the click-clack of the windshield wipers.

Once Russell looked back at the gold-toothed man. He sat across from Darcy. He just stared at her. She was reading a book.

Then Darcy pulled the cord to get off and started to go to the door. "See you tomorrow, Russell," she smiled. Russell held her arm as she climbed down the slippery wet steps. The gold-toothed man got off and headed down the street behind Darcy.

The bus took off. Russell was glad the man had gotten off the bus. But maybe he was being scared for nothing. Maybe "Mr. Gold-Tooth" wasn't interested in him at all. Suddenly he understood. Darcy! That man followed her off the bus! Russell yanked the cord. He jumped off the bus before it even stopped. He ran up the street after Darcy and the gold-toothed man. They were nowhere in sight. Russell stopped. Then he heard a crying voice.

"Don't. I don't have much money. Please let go of me." The voice was coming from some bushes next to the sidewalk. Russell pushed his way into the brush. The man with the gold teeth was pulling Darcy's purse away from her. When Darcy saw Russell, she screamed. Russell jumped on the man's back. Down he went with Russell right beside him. Darcy rolled to the side of the fighting men.

"Run, Darcy! Call the police," Russell yelled.

At first the gold-toothed man was on top,

Russell jumped on the man's back

choking Russell. Then Russell gave a jerk and he was on top. They rolled over and over. Russell finally pinned the guy just as the police got there and grabbed him.

Then the policeman said. "We've been after this guy for a long time. We think he works for the Mob. But we're not sure yet. This mugging will keep him in jail for awhile. But then he'll be out again. What we really need is to get *proof* that he's with the Mob." The officer told Darcy not to walk alone at night. Then he led the man away.

Russell put his arm around Darcy. "Come on. I'll walk you home."

"I'm so scared. I wish they could keep that awful man in jail." Darcy turned and put her head on Russell's chest.

It felt good. Russell walked her home. Then he headed toward the bus stop. He could tell the police about the $9500 and give them the black book filled with names. But what if they arrested him for the mugging?

But if he didn't tell, that man would be on the streets again. Darcy might be in danger. What a choice!

CHAPTER 9

The Catch

Russell walked to his room. He didn't even look behind once. The man with the gold teeth was in jail so he felt safe—at least for awhile. Inside his room, Russell took off his belt and laid the money on his bed. $9500. Was it worth being chased by the Mob? And Darcy. She was lucky tonight. Maybe next time he wouldn't be near enough to save her from that man. Jeez! What should he do?

Then Russell understood what was wrong. He was thinking like a Citizens' Convoy volunteer— like a nice guy. And that wouldn't work with crooks. He knew what he had to do. He climbed in bed and went to sleep right away.

Russell got up early the next morning. He put the money around his waist and the little black book in his shirt pocket. Then he went to St. Joseph's Hospital. He found out where Mrs.

Lawson was in the hospital. Then he went to the third floor. He stood at the doorway of the big room trying to spot her. There she was at the very end of the row of beds. He walked up to the side of her bed.

"Good morning, Mrs. Lawson. You're in a lot of trouble. Right?"

"You! You're the one who took my money!" She reached for the bell to call the nurse.

"I wouldn't do that," Russell said. "Not until you hear my plan."

"What plan? You took my money. Where is it?" Mrs. Lawson was shouting now.

"You'd better listen to what I say. Your life is in danger," Russell said.

"Wait. What do you mean? Are you with *them*?" Mrs. Lawson's voice shook.

"The Mob? No. But I know you're one of their bookies."

"They'll get me. They think I took the money. I've *got* to get it back to them." She reached out and grabbed Russell's hand. "Where is the money?"

"It's safe, Mrs. Lawson. Don't worry. It's still in the paper bag you left on the bus. I was chasing after you to give you back your paper bag."

Mrs. Lawson forgot about her pains and sat

"You'd better listen to what I have to say. Your life is in danger," Russell said.

up in bed. "Then you *didn't* mug me," she said.

"That's right," Russsell said. "So, Mrs. Lawson, this is the deal. I'll turn over the $9500 to you, but you have to tell the police who your collection man is."

"Are you out of your mind?" she said. "Why, he'd have me killed!"

"Not if he were in jail and you had police protection," Russell said. Then he told her about the man with the gold teeth and the scar on his face. "Is he your collector?" Russell asked Mrs. Lawson.

"Yes, he is," she said. "But no way am I going to tell the police on him."

"All right," Russell said, "if you don't turn the money over to the police to catch the collector, I'll give them this." He pulled out the little black book from his shirt pocket. "This is enough proof. He'll go free. You'll be in prison." Russell turned to go.

"Wait. Oh, dear. This is terrible. I'm just a helpless lady trying to earn a living," Mrs. Lawson said.

Russell cut in. "Make up your mind. Who goes to prison. Him or you?"

Mrs. Lawson asked, "And they won't send me to prison?"

"If you help to put the collector in jail, I'm sure the police will protect you. You might get lucky and get probation. You could do community service instead of going to jail."

Mrs. Lawson sat up in the bed. "You're right. Hand me that phone. I'll call the police right now. I'll be so glad when this is all over."

Russell handed her the telephone.

CHAPTER 10

A New Start

That morning on the bus, Russell told Darcy that the gold-toothed man was going to be staying in jail for a long time.

Darcy smiled. "Thank goodness. I was so scared last night."

Before Darcy got off the bus, she asked Russell to her home for dinner next week. "Mother wants to thank you, too, for helping me."

The next week, Russell had to report to his probation officer. When Russell got there, the probation officer was waiting. "Right this way, Mr. Newly," he said. "The judge will see you now."

Russell walked into the judge's office. He felt like he was taking his last steps of freedom.

The judge laid down the papers and looked up. "Sit down, Mr. Newly. I called you here because

"Sit down, Mr. Newly. "I called you here because I wanted to tell you how proud I am of you."

I wanted to tell you how proud I am of you. This report says that you have done a good job for the coffee shop. The Citizens' Convoy group is pleased with your work on the bus. How many more hours do you have to serve?"

Russell thought for a moment. "I don't know. At first I kept track of every minute, but then I got busy with some things and lost count."

"This report also states that you caught a mugger. You followed him off the bus and caught him trying to rob a young lady. This mugger is also a collector for the bookies," the judge said. "How did you know that man was a mugger?"

No way was he going to answer that one, Russell thought.

"Would you say," the judge smiled, "that it takes a mugger to catch a mugger?"

"Or maybe it was just luck, Judge," Russell answered.

"Keep up the good work, Mr. Newly. You're on your way to becoming a good citizen. Every city needs all the good citizens it can get. That's all." The judge stood up and shook Russell's hand.

Once outside the judge's office, he let out a deep breath. That was over! Now to go home and get cleaned up for dinner with Darcy and her mother.

Back at the rooming house he took a shower and put on his last clean shirt. He heard a knock on his door.

"Can I come in?" called Bob.

"Sure," said Russell, "but I'm going out in a little while."

"Heavy date?" asked Bob.

43

"Yep," said Russell, "I'm going to Darcy's house for dinner."

"Lucky," said Bob. "You're either smart or lucky. I'm not sure which."

"Maybe a little of each," answered Russell. "But, you know, Bob, ever since I started on the Citizens' Convoy, my luck, as you call it, has gotten better."

"I could use a little luck," said Bob. "Nothing has been going right for me. Nothing at all. I think I've lost my nerve. I don't even feel like going out and mugging anybody any more."

"You haven't lost your nerve," said Russell. "You've just gotten some good sense."

"Maybe, maybe not," said Bob.

"Listen," said Russell, "I know the right people now. How about trying the Citizens' Convoy? I'll bet if you sign up for that, the judge I know would help find you a job."

"A job?" said Bob slowly. "Boy, it's been a long time."

"Try it. You'll like it," said Russell.

"Okay," Bob said. "Let's talk about it tomorrow." He walked quietly out of the room and closed the door.

By golly, thought Russell, I think I've "caught" another mugger!